Hector

The Protector of The Six Realms

Creation of Ceryneia:

Book 1

Robin Alpine

Disclaimer

Please note the information contained within this document is for educational and entertainment purposes only. Every attempt has been made to provide accurate, up to date and reliable complete information. No warranties of any kind are expressed or implied. Readers acknowledge that the author is not engaging in the rendering of legal and financial, medical or professional advice. The content of this book has been derived from various sources. Please consult a licensed professional before attempting any techniques outline in this book.

TABLE OF CONTENT

The worlds had been free of war for almost ten years. Their enemies were finally at bay.

The nations who hated them and wanted to burn them down to the ground, had finally given up after their many futile attempts. The people were enjoying the freedom from constant fear of attacks.

The weather on this side was always bright and favorable, certainly one of the most loved parts of the worlds.

The beauty of the oasis was second to none, little wonder why they were the envy of other nations. The mash green fields and high mountains surrounding the "Worlds" as they are called made it nearly impossible for enemies to cross the line.

Despite this however, they had enemies always attacking every other year until the dragons took it upon themselves to be the shield and Protectors of the "Worlds".

They gathered themselves on the mountain tops and Practiced advanced defense skills, this training went on even in extreme weather conditions such as heavy downpour that soaked through their snout, seeped through their scales, and made their wings heavy as though they carried the mountains themselves. The training also was done in the peak of winter, where the dragons were made to sleep outside using only their scales as protection against the harsh winds and heavy snow.

For many dragons the nights were usually the hardest to go through, because the night came with uncertainty. It became the duty of the dragon race to be the Protectors of the Realms.

Everyone made way for the Dragons, leaving them alone to do their call. Everything they needed was provided for them from the national treasury of the Realms.

The people of the realms were naturally peace-loving people and shared everything with one another. Greed was a trait they never possessed, it was dealt with immediately it stirred up, maybe that was the reason for the bliss they enjoyed until the surrounding nations began to prey on them, forcing the Dragon clan to become Protectors.

Prior to this time, skilled labor was the sole duty of dragons and the clan delivered high class innovations for the Realms. Now another clan had taken over the affairs of skilled labor leaving the dragons to pay full attention to protection, since they were the strongest creatures of the Realms.

CHAPTER 2

"Brethren, today we ride! Today we take what is rightfully ours!"

The leader of the Gorgon army, Mungo, bark in his address to his soldiers and they cheer in agreement. His whole body shook as he spoke glaring into the bright clouds, he pointed to sky while he continues to address the soldiers.

"In a matter of hours, we'll take over the Worlds, we'll cast our dark shadows on their bright world. They will no longer see their precious daylight, the only thing that'll will greet them while they die is our fog casted sky. They took the only thing I held dear, the woman of my dream" he spat on a pile of grass beside him as though the gooey potent saliva was aimed at the one, he had a grudge against. "Today, we'll possess the good of their land. We will snatch everything from them down to their dreams, and because they will not see us coming, it will be like snatching candy from a baby."

As Mungo, the leader of the Gorgon army continued in his speech, their dark clouds begin to circle their hideout.

"They love the sunlight, they always celebrate and have taken the resources- crystals that are rightfully ours, today, we'll bring them clouds, they'll roll in the muds of our anger. We've camped quietly outside their city for the past ten years, plotting. Our surveillance teams have done great with the camouflage and today as they celebrate the eclipse, it'll be their last celebrations ever."

His speech excited the Gorgon army and they begin to prance with their horns clashing against one another. "They won't know what hit them!" He added.

The soldiers cheer on as they begin to suit up for war and the destruction of the Worlds.

The dark clouds that hovered around them went undetected by the World because on this year's Eclipse celebrations, there were no Protectors on the mountains because it's been over ten years without attacks or chaos, everything and everyone flourished. Today, every Protector was made to be home with their family and friends.

The Gorgon soldiers begin to parade the grounds in anticipation of the order to advance.

Mungo uses his spies at the watchtowers on the mountains to confirm before they advance. The advanced visionary equipment he had stolen from a black-market trader years back, always came handy for him I'm such situations.

He narrows his eyes through the green visionary equipment to ensure he was right. Satisfied he barks his order "advance!"

The Gorgon soldiers exchange mischievous glances as they match towards the Worlds.

This has been a long-standing grudge by the demon nations. One of the guardians of the Worlds had a long time ago fallen in love with Mungos betrothed from another Nation. Her father was king and had no other child. So, Mungo swiftly proposed to her family unconcerned whether she had someone else. When she rejected his offer and eloped with her lover, never to be seen again. Mungo was distraught and sort vengeance against any and everything related to the Worlds. So, taking over Cerynia was not just about the Gorgon Nation, it was a personal score he'd settle today. It was a personal battle.

CHAPTER 3

Since the dragons began protecting the kingdom, they've overthrown 10 Nations seeking to destroy them.

Every member of the clan is supposed to go through six months of separation and intense training immediately they're fifteen. So both male and female members of the Dragon clan undergo the same test to enable them defeat the enemies. The tests range from agile wing test, hooves assessment, clawing tasks, fire breathes, under water combat and more. The Protectors undergo rigorous trainings of endurance of harsh weather and hunger conditions as well because you'd hardly be able to tell the abilities of the opposition forces.

Cedric the leader of the army of Protectors of the Worlds ensures that all times the military force is fully equipped. Cedric keeps watch at one of the watchtowers on the mountains at the North end of the Worlds, and he's always the first to spot the enemies and alert his dragon army.

"I think we've worked very hard over the years. We've put our best foot forward for the Worlds and the Executive Council seeks to make The Day of the Eclipse our day of rest and relaxation". Cedric said as he addressed the small crowd gatherer around him.

Amulet, the youngest member of the team being addressed rushed in from outside trying to hasten up to meet up the debriefing.

"This awful, as much as I try not to call attention to myself, that's exactly what I end up doing. He thinks to himself. "Maybe I should change my morning routine"

Cedric immediately looks in his direction as if reading his thought, shaking his head in disappointment he asks Amulet.

"You're the youngest member of this team, how come you never report early for briefing?"

Before Amulet thought to respond, Cedric continued giving instructions of the Eclipse celebrations. "I Demand that everyone obey the decree by the Council. It is for our own good to unwind and join our families and the rest of the Worlds in celebration. Besides we've had peace and no opposition for the past 10 years. We've thought our enemies and those around us a lesson they will never forget in a hurry."

CHAPTER 4

"Shhh, we'll match quietly to the mountains, once within the World, Goo, let loose your ice goo. Make sure you engulf the length and breath of the Worlds in a bubble " Mangu said from above. He looked around the arena, trying to choose the weakest links, so he could send them back to their Nation for reinforcement just in case, they did not catch the Protectors off guard. "Chains go back to Gorgon for reinforcement and more armory".

As the Gorgon army marched into the mountains, thick clouds followed them with Goo a Demon gifted with making sticky goo that could hold anything hostage. It was the peak of the Eclipse celebrations, the sun and moon would collide any minute now and this was the best time to strike. Mangu thought to himself; we've laid watch for too long and I now I can taste victory in my mouth.

"Leap over the walls quickly, and surround the Worlds," Mangu instructed excitedly.

"We're an inch from victory, today, we'll take what's rightfully ours".

Every demon used his own gift as they entered the city, every path they crossed withered. The green fields took on their darkness that surrounded the Demon army, trees swayed away from them and fell off, even the wind stopped.

With Goo's ice bubble, the Protectors had weaker powers, their breathe could not penetrate the skyline. Even if they attempted to fly into the sky, thy could barely see a thing because of the thick fog from the demons. There was no escape for them- both mere citizens and Protectors.

There was no escape route as the fiercest dragons fought with all their might.

The Demon storm the arena causing chaos and in commotion people run to save themselves. The dragons shield some people with their wings. The Fylakto dragons stand together using their silver and gold glittering skin as a source of light to push back the demons and succeed in killing some demons before they're wiped out by the demons.

The Campe dragons enter into the battle arena, attempting to save their friends, but are unable to save themselves as they are engulfed into the Monstrous goo.

CHAPTER 5

Cedric swims through the large lake into the mouth of the hideout familiar to only dragons. This is a life and death situation as far as he was concerned. He reminded himself that this was the last resort for any Protector, he needed reinforcement. Surely, Irad the keeper of the cave must have something or know something that could be done. What if Irad was out when this attack took place, what would he do. He doubted it though considering the fact that Irad never too days off since he lost Saphira, his beloved wife.

The cave Underneath the mountain was a fortress. It held the martial books, the armoury and more secrets that only dragons knew.

As he emerged from the water clinging onto the his talon that had been wounded in the battle. He knocks on the door.

Iriad opens the door, suprise plastered all over his face, "Cedric, what happened to you" he asks as he urgently leads Cedric into the shelf area of the cave.

"we're under attack, Iriad. We let ourselves go without precaution and now we're under attack". While he still spoke, another knock came through.

Iriad rushed to the door only to find Ryex and Eurasto at the door, wounded as well.

"How did we let this befall us? How could we be so careless. Ryex said lost with sadness, his light purple scales becomes darker.

"I couldn't use my breath" lamented Eurasto.

"Neither could I" Ryex said.

"I need to consult from my archives" he was saying when he heard a alarm blast again. They all rush to the door to see who it was. It was Niar, a firece dragon of the Fylakto tribe. She was badly wounded her as her wings are badly burnt. "Quick, help her" Irad said motioning to the others.

"I couldn't use my breath", she mumbled "I tried to fly but the clouds burnt my wings" she added.

"It must be something in the air" Irad said. I have to check it out. He takes out an equipment, walks towards the window. He looks into the sky and sees the ice bubble.

CHAPTER 6

As Amulet emerged from under the cave, his neck is larger than usual, a little too large for his small frame, his usually leaf green skin begins to glimmer bluish green. His wings have taken on a darker shade of the colours all the dragons whose breath he now possessed and a calm yet brilliant light flashed from his eyes.

Amulet could not tell how he was feeling but he knew if the others were brave enough and trusted him enough to give their fire breathes to him, the he had to take full responsibility and save the Worlds even if it cost his life.

He is aroused from his thoughts when Irad winces from the pain on his left hooves after stepping on a trap set by the demons.

"I think I stepped on a trap" he says amidst his painful groans.

" Be calm, hold on tight, I'll get you out of this situation" Amulet tries to reassure Irad.

"Don't worry about me, I've lived a full life," Irad replied. He had no family even before this attack, his whole life had been to guide the caves and everything in it, so dying now was a sacrifice worth paying. "you have to carry on your mission, fulfil your destiny, go and save our beloved land. Salvage what is left before it is too late." He nudges Amulet away reassuring him to put an end to the chaos.

Amulet gets on his way towards the edge of the mountain where the Goo stood guarded by an legion. He moved stealthily in order not to be detected until he got close enough to set fire on the legion guarding Goo, the maker of the ice bubble.

As Amulet made his way up the mountains, he took one last look at Irad. He hadn't moved all the while, he just stood there in deep agony, his left hoove bleeding from the trap.

Irad stood there, his hoove bleeding " what a way to go" he said to himself. "At least I'll also died saving our Worlds". He murmured.

On sighting Amulet a part of the legion breaks out screaming as they advance towards him. He ebbs closer to the cliff. He sets a hoove on the mountain and another hoove on the land. With a loud War shriek peculiar to dragons, he ignites the legion guarding Goo. Stepping back, he balanced his weight on the foot on the mountain, my weight on my left foot, targeting the legion rushing towards him, he roars and the winds blow the legion off the mountain.

Mungo lands on the mountain with his air beast and tries to sway him. "Give up young dragon, you alone cannot defeat us. We're a

legion, for crying out loud". He scuffs at Amulet.

Amulet looking at him with his calm fiery eyes replies "I might be one, but I'm never alone".

"This is your last chance young dragon. I see you're special, join forces with us and rule the world alongside this great Nation." Mungo persuades.

Charging up his breathe of fire, he steadies himself, arching his back as one ready to pounce on a prey, and sets fire on more demons guarding the Goo.

Without his notice, a heavy metal blow lands on his hoove on the land, blinded by the pain, he turns towards the direct and another heavy blow lands on him, this time blinding his fiery right eye. Out of his left eye he could see Mungo, giving him more blows in succession, and his body was covered in blows making him unsteady. He fell towards the mountain, right into the middle of the legion guarding the Goo.

"This is my chance", he thinks through the excruciating pain.

Gaining momentum while he lay in their midst, he aims at Goo with his last fire breath, engulfing the Goo first. As Goo falls, the ice bubble shatters and the mountain begins to crack. In all his pain he crawls forward and sets the mountain ablaze. He crawls further to the cliff of the mountain, making sure that no demon escapes, some are trapped in a cave, he breaths fire engulfing himself too and Mungo.

As Amulet's as settles on the land, the green pastures, plants, flowers and trees become restored. The ashe from Amulet's scales become a healing balm on the worlds.

The Protectors had died saving their lives, now it was their turn to honor the Protectors. The citizens that survived formed a new council and began deliberating how to move on from such great destruction on the Worlds.

"It would not be good that the sacrifices our Protectors paid should be in vain" Tanu the head of the council lamented. "How do we pick up these pieces and move forward.?" He said with tears in his eyes.

Another member of the council then suggested they do away with the name "the

Worlds". "This name has caused us so much sorrow" he added. "We should name this Nation after our fallen heroes, for even in death, they Protect us."

The council coming to a consensus agree to name the Worlds Cerynea and named the Worlds Ceryneia. All gotten from the first letters of the names of the fallen Protectors-Cedric, Ryax, Eurasto urasto, Niar, Iriad and Amulet.

CHAPTER 7

Amidst the peace restored to the land of Cerynia, Hector found himself wandering through empty streets in broad day light. The streets were deserted, there was no sound of laughter, no street vendors to be seen anywhere, persuading passersby's to purchase their products. Two years after the restoration of peace and citizens were still afraid to go out, everything is now done remotely from their homes, thanks to the Trolls. The only footsteps on the curb are that of Hector and his beloved mammal, Pilot.

They made quite an interesting team. Hector the fifteen-year-old boy looked small for his age, five feet two inches tall, dressed in his regular clothes, khaki pants and khaki shirt. Both were faded from over use but fitted perfectly on his small frame. His feet held the most fashionable item he owned; Trail Blazer boots his mom got him as he turned 15. Trail Blazer boots are in vogue now, all the kids wore them because they were comfortable and sleek. On his belt was a whip, popularly called koboko, with three sharp bristles. His brunette hair was sleeked back into a ponytail at the nape of his neck, it framed his face, accentuating his deep brown eyes with a masculine nose and thin lips to match.

The mammal, Pilot, was a huge, four-legged beast. His big, oval shaped eyes were thoughtful yet fierce, set on a head shaped like that of a bull. He was brown with white spots; his nose was black; he had a strong tail that served as one of his survival mechanisms. He looked like a fierce creature beside the small framed Hector. It was often wondered how Hector could take such a wild looking mammal.

Taking a small alley that served as shortcut for him to get to the Ninjas training field. He hastens his steps in order to avoid being late. So far, he has proven to be stronger than boys bigger in size than he was. It was Ninja tradition that all the children from the realm begin training as warriors, especially now that the Protectors were few and mostly infants. In fact, it was his family's turn to bring a representative from the realm to guard the Nexus Mountain, where the demons were trapped after the attack.

Hector snuck into the arena. Amongst the boys his age training to be Ninjas, he had the thinnest frame. His hair in ponytail made matters worse as he was often mistaken for one of the girls. The whole realm had their doubt about his frame, he looked too frail, he was too small, would he be able to represent the realm in the protection of the Nexus?

By mow he was used to the doubt, the disapproving looks, the snide comments. Some time ago, an older ninja of the clan even said, it'll be better to send Pilot his mammal than to send him to represent the realm. If it were up to them, they'd even send a member of another family.

This is an opportunity to prove himself to his clan "they have to see that great things also come in small packages" he thought to himself.

CHAPTER 8

With his feet parallel and wide apart, back straight and knees pointing inwards, he was the first amongst his peers to do the Diba Dachi- it was a strenuous stance for beginners achieve, he had been practicing it in secret. It had taken a while to get it right, but he had put all his in. Pilot wiggled his strong tail with excitement as he watched.

The instructor of Diba Dachi, a warrior from Mimosa clan had an impressed look in her eyes, but of course a warrior never shows they're impressed by trainees. Although the sun shone in his eyes, he held his stance while everyone else battled with holding the position. It felt nice to have impressed the instructor, one thing was certain though: she seemed to have taken a liking to him

It was nice to have impressed this instructor, but then what about the others. He'll have to always try twice or three times as hard to ever impress them. This first year of ninja training really proved tough on him, even though he was better at everything. Maybe that's why the saying goes: to whom much is given, much more is expected.

"Take a break, guys. We'll continue in 20 minutes" the instructor said as she walked towards Hector. She had black long wavy hair that always seemed like she poured a bucket of water on just her head before leaving her house. She towered over Hector, looking at him intensely with her small brown eyes " you did great today kid" she said, smiling heartily at him. Her eyes were warm and friendly, and you know how they say the eyes are the channel to the soul.

Hector tried hard to hide his excitement "thank you Ma'am, I've practiced a whole to be able to hold the stance". Pilot sat close beside him. His instructor addressing Pilot says "I've heard so much about you, what tricks can you show me?"

Hector smiling, brings out three apples, hands them to his instructor and tells her to toss them, with a swift motion, she tossed the apples high up in the sky. Pilot jumped higher, retrieved the apples swiftly and lands on his hind legs. He wiggles his strong tail signifying his excitement to show off some more tricks. The instructor laughing pats his head.

"You see Hector, consistent practice is what leads to perfection" she said, still patting Pilot on the head. "I hope you're not in a hurry?" she asks.

"No ma'am, I hope I'm not in any sort of trouble?" Hector says, looking boldly at her.

"Far from trouble, in fact, I just want to say how impressed I am by your performance" she confessed. "I actually wrote you off due to other people's opinion of you, I'm glad I had my own encounter, in order to judge for myself. You're really working hard to prove that you deserve a place in the team of Mount Nexus protectors, and I'm sure you'll make the realm proud. Never doubt in yourself and in your abilities, no matter what anyone says or thinks".

Hector looks at her amazed, this is his first ever complement from an Instructor, or from anyone except his parents. This was a moment of reward for him. It was a small victory, but it was a victory still. Instructors gave words of encouragement to first year warriors a lot, however, the Diba Dachi instructors were a hard lot to please. No one outside their clan seemed to be able to perfect the stance. In fact, even established ninja warriors struggled with this class, and immediately discarded it once they passed the final class. The stance was a difficult one to hold and no one ever held it at first trial.

Finally gaining his speech, he thanked her "thank you ma'am" smiling heartily, he blurted out, "I'd never any complements from anyone except my parents, I'm really happy ma'am".

Pilot began making noises; he still had the apples, she'd thrown earlier. She tossed them up again, higher this time. Pilot looked at her with his oval eyes, as if saying, impressive, he leaped higher after all three apples, retrieving them in no time.

"Okay, big guy" she said, Patting Pilot and giving the retrieved apples another fling, this time with a Diba Duchi stance. The apples surprisingly go way higher than both Hector or Pilot expected. Pilot immediately leaps after the apples. Hector immediately takes his position beside her.

"You know the diba duchi is a thing of the mind, your mind has to be prepared and free of any intruding thought whatsoever. You've got to learn duba dachi as a way of life, that's what will make it easier. You did good by practicing, but you'll do better if you practice the stance as a way of life".

She makes a harder move with the stance that amazes Hector. "Also, you should call me Ms. Judy, ma'am makes me sound ancient" she added smiling. "Just keep doing your very best, I'm rooting for you, and very soon, everyone will see your good works".

CHAPTER 9

After the battle between the Gorgon nation and the Worlds ended, the Worlds was renamed Cerynia, after the dragons that paid the ultimate price of sacrificing their lives for their land. Irad was rescued by the survivors and became overseer of the unhatched dragon eggs found in the clan after the battle. The young dragons were hatched and are being trained under his supervision.

Cerynia was divided into six realms after the Big attack on the Worlds. It seemed unlikely that any other nation will try again to wage war against Cerynia because of their armed forces. They were now more equipped than they'd ever been in the past.

Cerynia is divided into six Realms, each realm specialising in something profitable for the collective good of the nation. Each realm was bountifully blessed in a skill which was crucial for the survival of Cerynia.

Cerynia was a lovely place that now needed not only a key to enter but also a digital pass code, thanks to the Trolls, who controlled the highly digitalized technology. It seemed unlikely that anyone would want to maul their Nation again after all that happened before. Everyone outside Cerynia knew they stood no chance. It was not a wise decision to wage war or be a threat due to their high tech and diverse gadgets.

The Realm of the Trolls was one of the most amazing sights. Everything was digitalized, the city walls were high up like a fortress. They looked plain, painted in washed out green and on the outside seemed ordinary. Once closer, unless you're from the troll realm the walls appear like a mirage. The closer one got to the Realm walls, the further away it seemed.

Their skills here were natural as they possed high intellectual capabilities. The Trolls had the biggest library and study center in all of Cerynia. Only Trolls had liberty to use the library, on rare occassions, visitors from other Realms were approved and allowed to seek knowledge from the Troll library and study center . There were Trolls from all works of life, their were artists, musicians, high caliber corporation but all operated a digital track and applied their high intellect to building safety to the other Realms.

Even among the highly intellectual Trolls, there are some set apart from the rest. They're called the special Trolls. The special Trolls attend a different school from the rest of the Trolls. This school is made for Trolls with bigger brains than the regular ones. Four years after their birth, they taken to their boarding school where they learn everything, they need to know the intellectual affairs of Cerynia. The designated teachers were from all of Cerynia but most in authority were also special Trolls. This year, they need to pick the best Troll to be part of the Protectors of the Nexus. According to the decree by the leaders of Cerynia, this selection is set to happen once every three decades, this system was implemented after the Attack and because the system is still new, the authorities of the Realm of Trolls had not yet figured out the exact way to go about the selection in their realm.

Looking around, the host of the Leaders meeting of the Special Trolls academy asks, "is there any particular student you all think is beyond exceptional?"

He suddenly realized that most of the leaders had their hands up, from experience, he knew this meant there was one person. "Yes, go ahead" he says pointing towards the third Troll from his right.

The Troll passes a clip board to him showing Lin's scores in all her Tests. The leader takes a look and asks "Does anyone object to this Linoy, is he as good as this report says?" No one answers but they all wear a funny look

look on their faces. "What's funny," he asked looking at the same Troll for answers. "Linoy is a she" the Troll says. Despite trying to hide the embarrassment, the green splotches on his blue overall blue skin give him away.

"Linoy is a she?" The leader asks without actually expecting any answers back.

"Well, if Linoy is as good as you all have said, I need to see her in action myself". He Continues, "Organize a pop challenge immediately, let's see how she performs if taken unaware.

Linoy walking to her next class unaware of what is to come, suddenly hears the commotion as everyone in scurries to the ball room where challenges are held. " isn't today meant to be free of practice, just when I was hoping to complete my plastic robot 5.0 invention.

"Lin, we're having a pop-up challenge now". Cheeky grumpily murmured behind her. Cheeky was her best friend who stood almost four feet shorter than she did, she was the only one that still calls her Lin. Her orange hair held in two pigtails. For a Troll Sanda was considered beautiful, she had magnificent blue skin, orange hair and freckles across her cheeks. The freckles on her cheeks seem to be highlighting her hair. She had all the he-trolls drooling after her. Linoy had always been the ugly friend when in this particular ship. She stood at 8 feet and she was barely even twelve. That's almost the height of a full blown adult troll, as if that's not bad enough, she had to have thin sleek silver hair that would unravel whenever she tried to style it differently. He-trolls didn't necessarily like like her but at least, they didn't totally hate her, even if they did, it wouldn't be because of her look, it'd just be because she's the best at robotics and all other things.

"Why do we have a pop challenge today?" Lin asked Cheeky. " Today is meant to be challenge free. I was hoping I'd finish up my newest invention today".

"Well, that's not happening today, obviously". Cheeky replied nudging her to sit.

"Hello students, apologies for cutting your day short". The head instructor was addressing them now. "Today's challenge will determine who will represent our Realm as Protector of

the Nexus. Ensure that you finish this task
speedily".

CHAPTER 10

"That's not the case here, Puck," Rada said. "We can use one - no, two, potions to create the spell. Get the rest of the potions so we can sort out which should be used for what".

"Thing is from my studies, I've come to a conclusions that we can use herbs instead of those chalky potions". Puck replied.

Rada looked into the oval shaped blue pot designated for spells like this. The pot seemed endless as his thoughts wandered, he wondered whether to listen to Puck's new ideas or just continue the way he knows. "Get the potions," he said, his face bleak.

As Puck went about sorting out the potions, Rada continued to stare into the endless bottom of the spell pot. "This lad is way too reckless, he thinks we older wizards do not or have not studied. With such recklessness, I hope he ends up being picked by the core six".

Puck has been Rada's apprentice since he turned ten, now that he turned 14 a week ago, it is almost time to ordinate him with the hat of wisdom. So he can be a Protector at the Nexus. Rada always worried about Puck and his visions. He hoped Puck will win, he even considered giving into this herbs idea because Puck seemed a lot wiser than his years.

Puck took the hot coal in his hand. "I think you'd be great for another spell, just not this one" he spoke to the coal. Immediately, the coal seemed to be drawing him into a fiery space. It's his regular trance where he sees a ninja drowning in the Nexus. This time he was able to ask the Ninja his name. "Hector" he murmured the name. He didn't quite understand the trance, neither did his master when he told him. True they were all wise here but even the necromancers couldn't interpret his visions.

"Very good mixture," Rada said. "I wasn't sure you'd completely obey me. Go on. You see, I agree with you, we need to incorporate new methods of spell preparation".

In the Realm of the wizards, there was constant consumption of books, several studies to show oneself worthy to be listened to. For them there was no showdown or battle for the Nexus keeper. There were simply designations. Each year of producing a representative, a family was designated and a suitable candidate is picked to start training from the age of ten, which is how Puck ended up training with Rada as his apprentice.

Puck was the third of five siblings and as the middle child was mostly left by himself. His gifts were rare as he could see visions and had a deep old soul. He was seen as wise beyond his years, so when the time came to pick a representative, there were no hesitations to choose Puck, as the representative.

CHAPTER 11

The green lands of the Knight Realm stretched across the plain. Beyond the horizons, the rosebuds with thorns stood as stockade surrounded the realm of Knights barricading intruders. After the Attack, they took the liberty of cascading the whole realm with stockade. The wind always carried the scents of wet soil as Knights always sort to plant.

In fact, the Knight society was operated on a class system. The more crops a family is able to produce put them higher on the social pedestal so everyone worked hard to increase their worth by doubling crop production annually. Despite this competition, the realm was very peaceful and Knights supported one another. The highest producers were ordained by the chief of the realm. The Realm was always in constant touch with the Trolls because they relied on agricultural technology to increase productions. They basically were the source of food for Cerynia.

Delia loved the wet soil odors ; she had smelled them often growing up in the hills of their realm. More than anything, she loved water. She loved to swim in the lakes and rivers that surrounded her home. She picketed her horse in a field within view as she went about applying fertilizers to her crops. There was the big crop showdown for her age grade. This was done in order to select a representative for the realm, as Protector of the Nexus. Whoever produced the largest crop on the showdown would be selected as Protector.

Inside her plants was untouched, the three foot stockade wall enclosed her plants, as she ploughed through she heard feet shuffling behind her. She did not want to be bothered by anyone now because she had to focus on her plant. Turning around, she lost her balance and almost fell but Hector was swift enough to hold her from falling. She hadn't expected to see anyone here, let alone a Ninja. Visitors were allowed in the realm but that mean one should creep behind her like that. Adjusting herself, she thanked him for his help and went about her work.

"That's a healthy plant," Hector judges, his face set. "Are they for the competition tomorrow?" He asked pointing towards a large corn cub that stood almost six-foot high. " now aren't you a good guesser" Delia said with a hint of mock amazement. "Why is a Ninja creeping through the farms?" Delia continued in her sing song voice. "I was just passing by and thought you needed help" Hector replied. "So you just go about the farms looking for who to help?" She said laughing, "you want to take the role of Knight in shiny armor from is Knights, yes." At this Hector also burst into laughter, "well, I was only trying to help, but since you do not need my help, I'll be on my way". At that he finds his way back the same way he came.

As Delia's placed her plant in the hall that looked like a farmers market from the numerous plants from competitors. Her heart beat fastened. She could see better plants than hers, and although her mother gave her the potion bloomindale, she was still skeptical. Obeying the instructions given to contestants to kick-start, she patted her good luck petal on her hair "good luck, dear", she murmured to herself.

"You may now begin" the voice of the announcer roared from the speakers. She went to work immediately, sprinkling a touch of bloomindale here and there and hoeing weeds off all at the same time.

After an hour, the bells chimed for the end of the competition. The judges let out the hoives to take out weak plants. Hoives was an agricultural technology created by the Trolls. Hoives were always used in this realm to take out weak plants. Fortunately, her plant was the only one still staying tall after the rummage.

"We have a winner," the voice from the speaker blasted through. "Delia, of the house of Hemstad, congratulations, you'll be representing our Realm at the Nexus. Make us proud, Dear girl."

CHAPTER 12

There were no white clouds in the sky because white cloud was potent for healing. The sky was an endless blue blanket stretched across the sky. There were several black birds chirping happily as they flew across the sky; a mash of green field underneath. There were a few trees on the small path. The lineup of horse moving slowly through the path seemed practiced. Their hooves against the ground made an effortlessly rhythmic echo.

This selection journey has taken them through several Realms, places they'd never have gone. They were all aware of the other Realms but no one seemed to venture out except the leaders and those that worked in aviation.

Hector wondered to himself why the Trolls didn't just give them one of the air trolleys or even one of the botts for land. Why did they have to travel by horses but he didn't want to complain about it, just that he thought movement would have been faster had they used the air trolley. Now they were in the Realm of Elves, to select the Elf that would join in the Protectors of the Nexus.

" We're here," echoed the voice of their guide. "Let's fit ourselves into the lounge in the order we usually do". Another day, another selection process, Hector thought to himself. Over the course of this selection journey, Hector's education and passion for the realms- for Cerynia had increased remarkably. He loved Cerynia very much, but now it was much more than he imagined. He knew how to track down anything or anyone he put his mind to. Even in cases were magic is used to hide passage or where appearances are shifted using Crystals, he could simply tell. He learnt this from the wizard's.

Before they arrived the Realm of the Elves, Phil had already been selected to be the realm's representative at the Nexus. He was the most qualified candidate as he had exceptional healing powers. Right from his early days, he had been seen as the best healer, healing small plants, scrubs and even insects.

The Elves were the healers, the biggest of them could catch white clouds from the sky and make herbal mixtures with them. The cloud herbal mixtures were used for more intense curing or even giving life. The whole of Cerynia depended on them for all medical aids, they were seen as both doctors.

By the time Phil got his pointy ears, he was already catching white clouds. No one taught him, it was natural instinct for him. This was a rare ability for Elves. Even the Elves that caught white clouds go through rigorous training to attain that height. It was rare that a teenage Elf would be able to catch clouds like that. Phil could also draw blue clouds if he wanted. He had supreme abilities and that was why, it was natural that he'd be the candidate selected for Nexus protection.

CHAPTER 13

Irad was the keeper of the books when the attack took place. After he got trapped in a Gorgon boogie, he urged Amulet to carry on without him, after all he couldn't even battle. When the battle ended, he was rescued and treated by the Elves before moving on to his Realm. The dragons had been the only Protectors but now the only dragons are babies. The eggs laid by dragons before the attack on the worlds is all that was left. He hands to nurture them until they hatched. The oldest of the young Dragons was three.

Petals sprang to her feet and bolted towards Hector, as the Protectors stepped into Irad's Castle. She was the oldest of the baby dragons, and was named Petals because her scales looked like rose Petals. Hector tried to duck but it was too late, they both crashed into the bookshelf nearest to the door. "Sowee," she said giggling, "I'm twrying out my feathers, am a bird" she said still giggling. "Petals, you're not a bird, you're a dragon, and stop bothering our guest" Irad cautioned.

She was a deep shade of pink, like she basks in the sun frequently. Her scales were shaped like rose Petals, her hoove was light brown and thick. She actually looks like a big bird, Hector, thought. She seemed to have read his mind because she starting to fly in circles in front of him. "Am a twit twit bird" Petals sang gleefully as she circled round Hector. The others just laughed at her especially at how she spoke. Her baby tongue did not allow her speak clearly.

Petal took a liking to Hector especially and he too liked her. She was the oldest of the little dragons so she helped Irad out with her smaller cousins. Having learnt to control and flap her wings, she taught the other close to her age how to flap wings and lift themselves up.

They had been at the castle almost three weeks now, but no form of collective training had even began. Hector kept thinking maybe they wanted to catch them awares.

Irad had been planning to commence the training but he wanted the Protectors to rest from the rigorous journeys they've had. He also wanted

It was nearly sunset on the fourth day of the third week they arrived. Irad and the other instructors gathered the Protector (names and their realms). when they had gathered Irad addressed them. "Welcome to my castle Protectors" irad said. "You've all been selected by your various Realms to come for the Protection of the Nexus. Take your time, enjoy the kingdom, tomorrow training starts fully."

CHAPTER 14

When trainings kicked off fully in the morning, Irad gave instructions to the Protectors. "I know you were told in your various Realms that you'd be made to battle against one another and the winner becomes the Protector of the Mount Nexus." He said in a very formal tone. "Well, that's not exactly how it works. It's true there's just one coronated Protector, however, the rest of you are going to be in his team because no one is an Island. We picked the best of you so you can contribute your gift in the protection of the Nexus. Protecting the Nexus is a big responsibility and I want you all to take it seriously.

They were taken to the arena by the instructors. They began by showing them through the barracks, the mess hall, and storehouses. In the mess they were introduced to the dignitary Lord Wyldon, the Commander of the league of Specials from the Troll Realm. He seemed oblivious of their presence. They could barely tell whether or not he saw them. The instructor carrying them round assured them that was the way he treated everyone that had a status less than his. It didn't matter at all I you were handpicked by Irad himself. As long as you held a lower badge, you were oblivious.

On their second day of training. They were all asked to report to the drawing Chambers during lunch break. When they arrived, they were greeted by the uniform maker. Delia, Lin and Petals were fitted by a female uniform maker from the Realm of Trolls, while Hector,

Phil and Puck were fitted by a Male uniform maker.

Irad gave instructions to the Uniform makers while he sat down at desk looking through pages of a technical book. "Leave some allowance in the sleeves and legs, because Lin seems to keep growing" he motioned to the Uniform maker as she took Lin's measurements.

When it was Delia's turn, he barely looked up from his and when it was Petals turn, he motioned for her uniform to take her exact form. Covering her wings and her tail. The uniform was to be made in such a way that the petals on her skin could still hide through.

"Make Hector's sharp at the breastplate so it can fit his sword. Add a pouch too at the waist for a penknife and a dagger. Ensure that Phil and Puck had pockets in their combat suits where they would store their potion and spell bottles". He gave further instructions and left the Chambers.

Their Uniforms would be ready the following week of the training. This training would last three long months before they headed for the Nexus.

CHAPTER 15

The leaves had begun to turn brown, showing it was almost time for the eclipse celebration. The difference now was that the celebration was not so much a celebration anymore. It was the time to reflect and remember the sacrifices made by the Dragons that saved the Worlds birthing Cerynia.

Delia and Lin shared a room while Petals went back to her hall where the other young dragons lived in Irad's Castle.

All through the day's lessons, Delia imagined soaking herself in hot water when she got back to the room she shared with Lin. In all, the bath-house was her favorite spot in here since there were no rivers or lakes within the barracks, she had to settle for what was available. Another place she loved was the garden. It always looked magnificent, she once told Lin that the waters and plants spoke to her, which she considered a half lie because the plants or water didn't use actual words. She just had an emotional attachment to them.

Hector is given the responsibility to give Petals flying lessons during their evening runs. She seemed to be catching up fast and it made him happy. As much as he like to teach Petals to flap her wings, the highlight of his day was usually watching Delia do her thing with plants in the garden. She looked the most peaceful and content in the gardens. He liked her. In fact, he liked-liked her, but he has to keep it to himself because he didn't think Delia would like him back.

Hector remember first meeting Delia during his first trip outside his realm. Puck and he met in the bursary building at the capitol, where an instructor picked them up so they could begin their journey picking up the other competitors. He rode in an air trolley for the first time together with Puck. Lin joined them at the Realm of the Knights. Their friendship was immediately. They clicked organically, as though they had known one another before now.

The evening runs always tired Puck out, probably because he wasn't cut out for running. His running partner was Phil. Phil loved to keep fit, so he liked to run. Prior to this time Puck didn't know Elves could even sweat, he never really looked at their anatomy in his books. Now he was learning a lot more about Elves in person. He shared a hall-like room with Phil and Hector. They were both really cool and he was surprised how they all got along so easily despite the diversities of their respective realms.

At night they all ate at the mess. It was time for them to unwind from the stress of each day. Phil loved to eat, he'd always ask for more food leaving the others clear on the joke about the Elves being the biggest benefactor of the knights agricultural prowess. He liked the team a lot because they were always cooperative. Despite the short time they've known themselves, they felt like family already.

In the mess, they greeted each other boisterously. They met other trainees in the barracks, some were training to be special agents, some wanted to join healers. The barracks were open for Cerynians from all six realms. However, Hector and his team were the youngest people in the mess. They were treated differently and called special. Hector himself was called the Protector by all and sundry. The others were simply addressed by name.

They headed for the servers' line without looking to see who was there. Hector watched Delia, feeling a little odd. She looked radiant, her pale skin looked nearly pink. The Knights were really the most good looking, he thought to himself. He watched her put her tray down while the service botts filled them with her preferred dish. He knew immediately that he had a crush on her- but couldn't be distracted by such thoughts- yet he felt pangs in his chest. Pangs of both happiness and pain.

CHAPTER 16

The trip to Mount Nexus was a hard one. Outside the moutains held a thick rainforest. There was constant rainfall in the area that had turned the roads into rivers of slippery mud that deepened with every step. Petals rode above them breaking the trail as she went, while Hector and the rest of the team made the journey on foot. Hector worried about her arriving first and touching something but he tried not to show his feelings.

Some weeks before he had instructed her on combat since her Realm had the original Protectors. She needed to know how to combat in case the need ever came. She did great with combat and he was very impressed. He tried to push the thought out of his mind that she'll touch anything. She was five but she was strong and mature enough to handle herself, after all she trained other younger dragons to fly. Inside the Rainorest, he checked to see what time it was, it mid-morning already. The group seemed tired from dodging mud and water puddles. Everyone was dirty because some fell into mud ditches on the way and the others always helped pull them out.

When they eventually arrived the Mount Nexus, the Instructors were there already as they came in their air trolley. They gave the instructions to the team. Asking them to ensure they stay at least twelve feet away from the mouth of the rock that held the Gorgons captive. They were meant to take turns watching the Mount with the longest watch time being twelve hours for Hector and the other twelve hours to be shared between Lin, Puck, Delia and Phil. Petals didn't have watch time, she could keep watch with anybody.

"If you have any challenge, ring the bell. There're digital acoustics that will enable us detect the problem and send help immediately. Ensure that you rest and do only the number of hours assigned to you. This is very important!" the lead Instructor concluded. The instructors get back on their air trolley and head back to their centers leaving Hector and his team to handle business.

"Now that they've left, we should get to work immediately" Hector said to his team.

"This zeal is a good thing but you heard the instructors say we must rest" Phil stated with a look of displeasure.

"I know what they said and it is the exact instruction I'm following" Hector retorted in a nearly irritated tone. "Let's all calm down. Hector, we need to rest a bit before we begin the watch, we all need rest". Delia said pointing at Petals that was already fast asleep in a nearby cave.

"I know that the Protection of the Mount Nexus lies on my shoulders, that's why you all want to rest and keep the mountain unattended. No problem. You can all relax, after all, wizard philosophers say; uneasy lies the head that wears the Crown". He looking sternly at Puck.

"Don't be that way, even you need rest. Your feet must ache from all that walking" Puck countered pointed at Hector's legs.

"You know what, I hate how nonchalant you all are concerning this. It's really getting on my nerves" Hector added angrily. "Take it easy man" Lin said sensing the uneasiness that had swooped into this conversation. She barely spoke, she mostly just listened to whatever anyone had to say. She had to intervene in this discussion before it got out of hand.

"Alright. I see that you're all on the same side. Well, just do as you please because I no longer care. Afterall I'm the Protector and you're all my subordinates. I don't need any of you!" He yelled and stormed of in the direction of the rock that held the imprisoned Gorgons.

CHAPTER 17

The Gorgons seemed to when there was a switch outside. They tried to get into the head of whoever was to guard the Nexus especially when they're new comers. They try this on and on and on with the hopes that one day, they'll escape this fiery pit and take their revenge once more on Cerynia.

Today actually seemed like a lucky day for them. There's the scent of innocence and anger coming from outside. It was saw intense because this scent wasn't even twelve feet away. It was about 8 feet away from this rock. "If whoever has that scent is hypnotized, he'll get us out of this hell hole" The voices whispered.

His time there was slow and he could barely keep his eyes open on the watch. He remembered his training in his Realm and how good he was. How everyone that didn't believe in him now marveled. He had achieved a lot in this short time. He'd prove to his team that he knows what's best for them. He had to show them he's the leader.

Barely three hours later, Puck is drawn into a trance. The same trance where he met Hector before they met physically. The only difference is this time, Hector was dinning at the Gorgons table surrounded by a burning furnace. "Guys, something is wrong" he yelled as he forced himself out of the trance. "Hector is in grave danger. We are all in grave danger".

The team dispersed to find Hector. Petals takes an ariel view and finds him struggling very close to the mouth of the rock that held the Gorgons. She immediately notifies the others and they all storm the Nexus. Puck reminds them that, they are meant to be at least 12 feet from the rock, else they'd all be hypnotized.

"Good thing I'm here" Lin said. She was the tallest of them all, not only because she was a Troll but also because she was the best with troll technology but also because she was the tallest in the team. She immediately carved out a piece of plastic that would cover the remaining 4 feet she didn't reach. Plastic was handy because it could melt and couldn't be possessed. She attached the plastic robot glove to her hand while the others tied a rope around her waist and waited for the instruction to pull.

"Pull!" She yelled as she grabbed Hector by both legs. The team pulled as hard as they could but Hector was too far away. Lin's robot glove started to melt from all the heat from underneath the Rock.

Hector was trapped in an in-between phase. He fought hard against the rock and fought hard against the trying to pull him out.

With one heavy pull just before the gloves bursted into flames, Hector was rescued.

He was hysterical and could not be controlled. Phil made a potion from white clouds he has caught on their way to the Nexus Mountain. Now the cloud that was darkening became started becoming stable again.

When Hector recovered the next day, he explained to the team that he could only remember himself dreaming. It was obvious that it wasn't just a dream.

CHAPTER 18

The Demons were beaten, defeated in fact but were stubborn creatures who never gave up. They always sort a seemingly weaker link to let them loose or enable them sow their evil oats. Hector's encounter with them emboldened him. He had seen the inside of their world when he was hypnotized. He still saw the lazer red fire in his dreams. Around the period of Celebrations was when they sort to free themselves. That was the perfect time because Hector was distracted. He had his mind wandering from place to place and although his team pulled him out of his trance, he couldn't help thinking how everyone would have been right that he isn't the one.

Hector hadn't faced the team since the event. "Hector? Leaves?" Petals babbled as she sat close to him handing him healing leaves Phil collected for him. The others had come into the cave and sat silently, no one speaking. "The leaves will stop your hallucinations" Phil said looking from Hector to the others.

Hector bit into one leaf, squeezed his face from the bitter sting that filled his mouth. "Thanks Phil. Thanks guys for coming at the time you did. I am sorry for what I said to all of you".

"It's, fine." They choruses. There was a sudden relief as they were sure he had learnt the hard way. He nearly let his ego ruin Cerynia again. Good thing Puck saw the vision immediately Hector left them after his outburst the previous afternoon.

"We're glad to have you back". Delia said looking up from the puzzle in her hands. "More than a team, we're friends, in fact we're the only family we have for now, so it's important we look out for one another". Everyone thought Delia was amazing. She always had the right words or knew the perfect word of comfort to use at the right time.

"I've learnt that the most important thing is that we're a team", Hector said. "What affects one person affects us all, and adversely affects Cerynia". I've learnt this the hard way and despite being the leader of this team, we're all friends and that's all that really matters. I'm sorry I let my ego get the best of me" the moment the words were out of his mouth, the whole team gathered round in a group embrace, their friendship toughened by their collective experience.

www.ingramcontent.com/pod-product-compliance
Lightning Source LLC
Chambersburg PA
CBHW031800150726
47989CB00006B/2806